Whoosh and Chug!

For Oscar and Leo. S.B.

First published in paperback in Great Britain by HarperCollins Children's Books in 2012

10 9 8 7 6 5 4 3 2 1

ISBN: 978-0-00-742529-7

HarperCollins Children's Books is a division of HarperCollins Publishers Ltd.

Text and illustrations copyright © Sebastien Braun 2012

Visit our website at: www.harpercollins.co.uk

Printed and bound in China

Whoosh and Chug!

by Sebastien Braun

HarperCollins *Children's Books*

Chug!

Chug!

Chug!

This is Chug. Hello, Chug!
He is a very busy little engine.

Every day Chug works hard collecting
and delivering heavy cargo.

Chug!

Chug!

Chug!

He might be slow, but he is very careful.

One morning, while the other trains were still asleep, Chug had to set off early for work.

Chug!

Chug!

Chug!

Whoosh, the passenger train, opened his eyes. "Catch you up later, slow coach!" he called out.

Chug went slowly on his way,
into the forest...

past the lake...

and through the tunnel.

Chug!

Chug!

Chug!

He stopped at the station to make a delivery, and then he went on.

Eventually Chug
reached the junction.

"Stop!"
cried Sigmund, the signal box.
"There's danger on the line ahead.
Wait for the green light, then you
can move on to the safe track."

Rumble...

Rumble...

Rumble...

As Whoosh sped along, he heard the
rocks begin to creak and groan...

Chug was still waiting at the lights
when he heard Whoosh calling out.
"I'm coming!" he yelled back.

Chug! Chug! Chug!

Chug bravely made his way down the dangerous track towards the cries for help.

Using his crane, he tidied
the rocks off the track,

slowly and carefully,

one by one,

until his carriages were
completely full...

and Whoosh was free at last!

"Thank you, Chug. I was *so* scared," said
Whoosh, reversing down the track.

Together the two friends started to make their way back home.

"You must be more careful next time, Whoosh," said Sigmund as they passed by. "We don't want any more accidents."

"I promise," said Whoosh.

"Thank you for being such a good friend," said Whoosh, once they were safely settled in the sidings. "You might have to work slowly, but you are very quick to come to the rescue!"

Chug smiled at Whoosh...

Chug!

Chug!

Chug!

"It's all in a day's work," he said.